THE SEA KING'S DAUGHTER

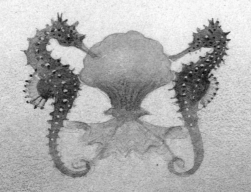

THE SEA KI DAU

Retold by
Aaron Shepard

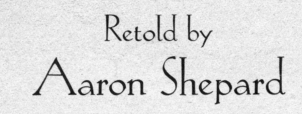

Illustrated by
Gennady Spirin

NG'S
GHTER
A RUSSIAN LEGEND

ATHENEUM BOOKS *for* YOUNG READERS

For Zanne
—A. S.

For my friends
—G. S.

HOW TO SAY THE NAMES

Novgorod ～ NOV-go-rod

Sadko ～ SOD-ko

gusli ～ GOOSE-lee

Volkhova ～ VOLE-ko-vah

Volkhov ～ VOLE-kove

Long ago in the river port city called Novgorod the Great, there lived a young musician named Sadko.

Every day, a rich merchant or noble would send a messenger to Sadko's door, calling him to play at a feast. Sadko would grab his twelve-string *gusli* and rush to the banquet hall. There he would pluck the strings of his instrument till all the guests were dancing.

"Eat your fill!" the host would tell him later, pointing him to the table and passing him a few small coins besides. And on such as he was given did Sadko live.

Often his friends would ask him, "How can you survive on so little?"

"It's not so bad," Sadko would reply. "And how many men can go to a different feast each day, play the music they love, and watch it set a whole room dancing?"

Sadko was proud of his city, the richest and most free in all Russia. He would walk through busy Market Square, lined with merchants in their stalls and teeming with traders from many lands. He never crossed the square without hearing tongues of far-off places, from Italy to Norway to Persia.

Down at the piers, he would see the sailing ships with their cargos of lumber, grain, hides, pottery, spices, and precious metals. And crossing the Great Bridge over the River Volkhov, Sadko would catch the glint from the gilded roofs of a dozen white stone churches.

"Is there another such city as Novgorod in all the world?" he would say. "Is there any better place to be?"

Yet sometimes Sadko was lonely. The maidens who danced gaily to his music at the feasts would often smile at him, and more than one had set his

10

heart on fire. But they were rich and he was poor, and not one of them would think of being his.

One lonely evening, Sadko walked sadly beyond the city walls and down along the broad River Volkhov. He came to his favorite spot on the bank and set his gusli on his lap. Gentle waves brushed the shore, and moonlight shimmered on the water.

"My lovely River Volkhov," he said with a sigh. "Rich man, poor man— it's all the same to you. If only you were a woman! I'd marry you and live with you here in the city I love."

Sadko plucked a sad tune, then a peaceful one, then a merry one. The tinkling notes of his gusli floated over the Volkhov.

All at once the river grew rough, and strong waves began to slap the bank. "Heaven help me!" cried Sadko as a large shape rose from the water. Before him stood a huge man, with a pearl-encrusted crown atop a flowing mane of seaweed.

"Musician," said the man, "behold the King of the Sea. To this river I have come to visit one of my daughters, the Princess Volkhova. Your sweet music reached us on the river bottom, where it pleased us greatly."

"Thank you, Your Majesty," stammered Sadko.

"Soon I will return to my own palace," said the king. "I wish you to play there at a feast."

"Gladly," said Sadko. "But where is it? And how do I get there?"

"Why, under the sea, of course! I'm sure you'll find your way. But meanwhile, you need not wait for your reward."

Something large jumped from the river and flopped at Sadko's feet. A fish with golden scales! As Sadko watched in amazement, it stiffened and turned to solid gold.

"Your Majesty, you are too generous!"

"Say no more about it!" said the king. "Music is worth far more than gold. If the world were fair, you'd have your fill of riches!" And with a splash, he sank in the river and was gone.

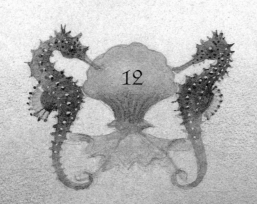

12

The next morning, Sadko arrived at the market square just as the stalls were opening. He quickly sold the golden fish to an astonished merchant. Then hurrying to the piers, he booked his passage on a ship leaving Novgorod that very day.

Down the Volkhov the ship sailed, across Lake Ladoga and the Gulf of Finland, and into the Baltic Sea. As it sped above the deep water, Sadko peered over the rail.

"In all the wide sea," he murmured, "how can I ever find the palace?"

Just then, the ship shuddered to a halt. The wind filled the sails, yet the ship stood still, as if a giant hand had grasped it.

Some of the sailors cursed in fear, while others prayed for their lives. "It must be the King of the Sea!" the captain cried. "Perhaps he seeks tribute—or someone among us."

"Do not be troubled," called Sadko. "I know the one he seeks." And clutching his gusli, he climbed the railing.

"Stop him!" shouted the captain.

But before any could lay hold of him, Sadko jumped from the ship and plunged below the waves.

Down sank Sadko, down all the way to the sea floor. The red sun shone dimly through the water above, while before him stood a white stone palace. Sadko passed through a coral gate. As he reached the huge palace doors, they swung open to reveal a giant hall.

The elegant room was filled with guests and royal attendants—herring and

sprats, cod and flounder, gobies and sticklebacks, sand eels and sea scorpions, crabs and lobsters, starfish and squid, sea turtles and giant sturgeon.

Standing among the guests were dozens of maidens—river nymphs, the Sea King's daughters. On a shell throne at the end of the hall sat the Sea King and his queen.

"You're just in time!" called the king. "Musician, come sit by me—and let the dance begin!"

Sadko set his gusli on his lap and plucked a merry tune. Soon all the fish swam in graceful figures. The seafloor crawlers cavorted. The river maidens leaped and spun.

"I like that tune!" declared the king. He jumped to the center of the hall and joined the dance. His arms waved, his robe swirled, his hair streamed, his feet stamped.

"Faster!" cried the king. "Play faster!"

Sadko played faster and the king's dance grew wilder. All the others stopped and watched in awe. Ever more madly did he move, whirling faster, leaping higher, stamping harder.

The Sea Queen whispered urgently to Sadko, "Musician, end your tune! It seems to you the king merely dances in his hall. But above us, the sea is tossing ships like toys, and giant waves are breaking on the shore!"

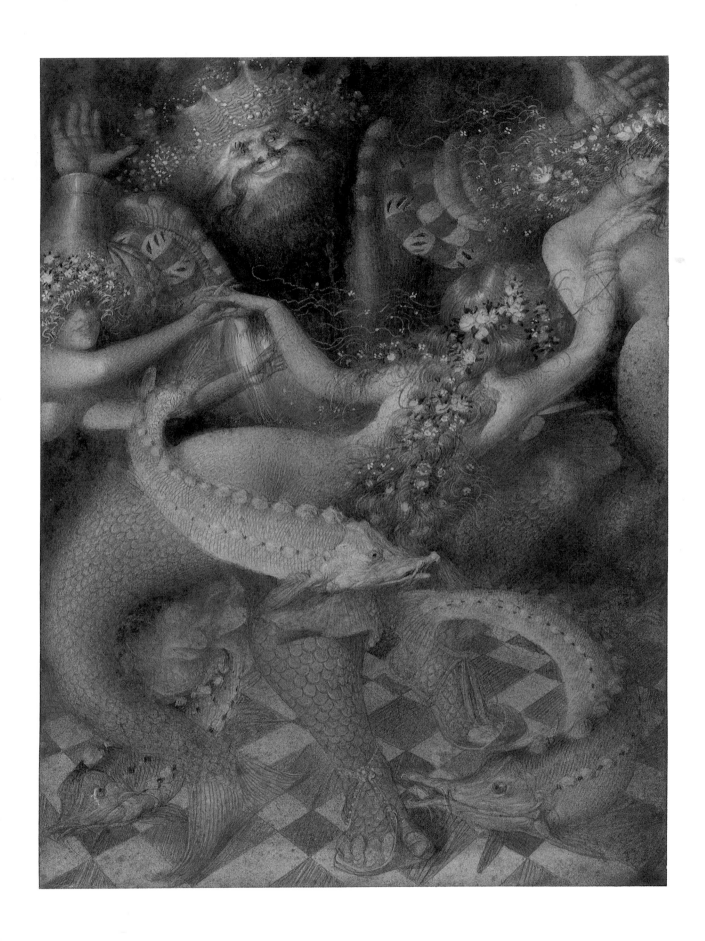

Alarmed, Sadko pulled a string until it snapped. "Your Majesty, my gusli is broken."

"A shame," said the Sea King, winding to a stop. "I could have danced for days. But a fine fellow you are, Sadko. I think I'll marry you to one of my daughters and keep you here forever!"

"Your Majesty," said Sadko carefully, "beneath the sea, your word is law. But this is not my home. I love my city of Novgorod."

"Say no more about it!" roared the king. "Prepare to choose your bride. Daughters, come forth!"

The river maidens passed in parade before Sadko. Each was more lovely than

the one before. But Sadko's heart was heavy, and he barely looked at them.

"What's wrong, musician?" the king said merrily. "Too hard to choose? Then I'll wed you to the one who fancies you. Behold the Princess Volkhova!"

The princess stepped forward. Her green eyes were sparkling, and a soft smile graced her lips. "Dearest Sadko, at last we can be together. For years I have thrilled to the music you've played on the shore."

"Volkhova!" said Sadko in wonder. "You're as lovely as your river!"

But the Sea Queen leaned over and said softly, "You are a good man, Sadko, so I will tell you the truth. If you but once kiss or embrace her, you can never return to your city again."

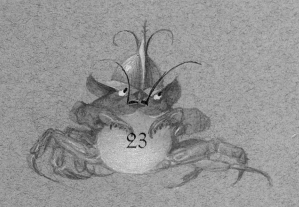

23

That night, Sadko lay beside his bride on a bed of seaweed. She's so lovely, thought Sadko, so charming—all I ever hoped for. How can I not hold her? But time after time, the queen's words came back to him—*never return to your city again*—and his arms lay frozen at his sides.

"Dearest," asked the princess, "why do you not embrace me?"

"It is the custom of my city," Sadko stammered. "We never kiss or embrace on the first night."

"Then I fear you never will," she said sadly, and turned away.

When Sadko awoke the next morning, he felt sunlight on his face. He opened his eyes and saw beside him not the Princess Volkhova but the River Volkhov. And behind him rose the walls of Novgorod!

"My home," said Sadko, and he wept—perhaps for joy at his return, perhaps for sadness at his loss, perhaps for both.

The years were good to Sadko. With the money that remained to him, he bought a ship and goods enough to fill it. And so Sadko became a merchant, and in time, the richest man in Novgorod. What's more, he married a fine young woman and raised a family. Many a feast he would hold so he could play his gusli and watch his children dance.

Yet sometimes still on a quiet evening he would walk out of the city alone, sit on the bank, and send his tinkling music over the water. And sometimes too a lovely head would rise from the river to listen—or perhaps it was only moonlight on the Volkhov.

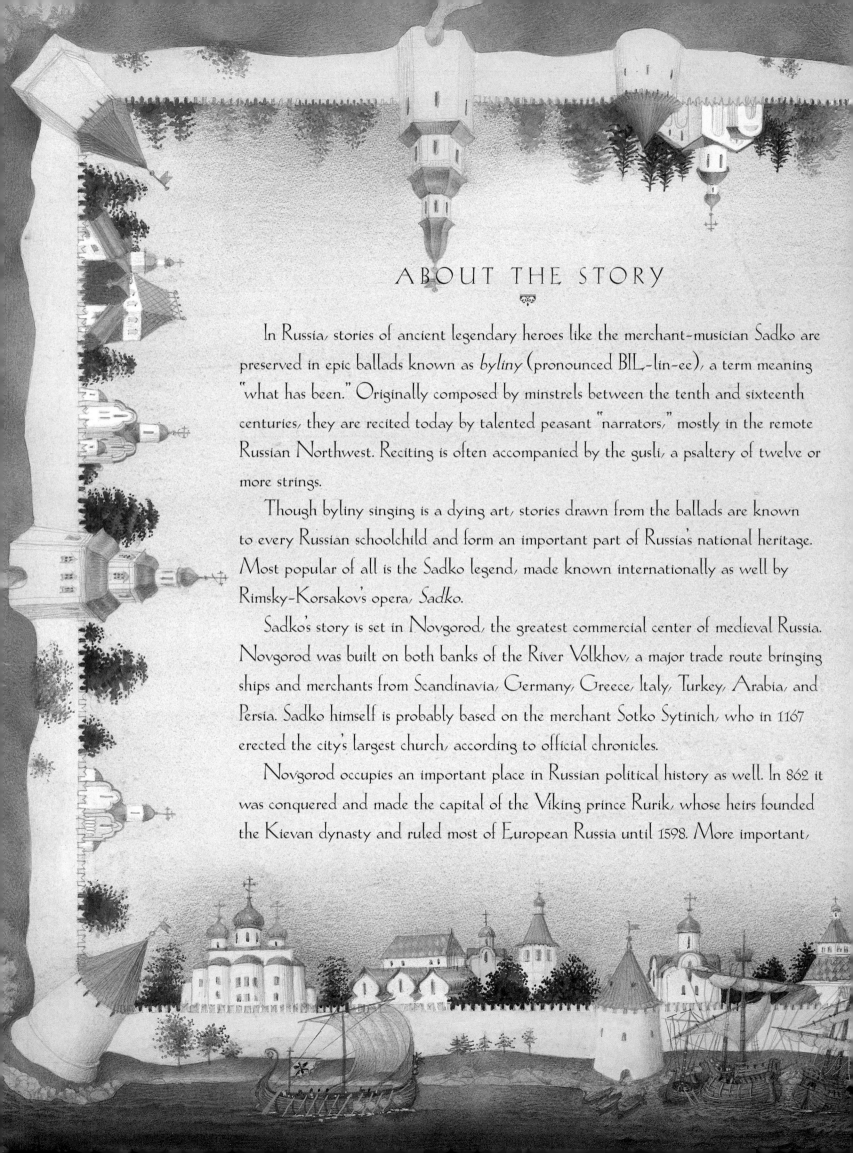

ABOUT THE STORY

In Russia, stories of ancient legendary heroes like the merchant-musician Sadko are preserved in epic ballads known as *byliny* (pronounced BIL-lin-ee), a term meaning "what has been." Originally composed by minstrels between the tenth and sixteenth centuries, they are recited today by talented peasant "narrators," mostly in the remote Russian Northwest. Reciting is often accompanied by the gusli, a psaltery of twelve or more strings.

Though byliny singing is a dying art, stories drawn from the ballads are known to every Russian schoolchild and form an important part of Russia's national heritage. Most popular of all is the Sadko legend, made known internationally as well by Rimsky-Korsakov's opera, *Sadko*.

Sadko's story is set in Novgorod, the greatest commercial center of medieval Russia. Novgorod was built on both banks of the River Volkhov, a major trade route bringing ships and merchants from Scandinavia, Germany, Greece, Italy, Turkey, Arabia, and Persia. Sadko himself is probably based on the merchant Sotko Sytinich, who in 1167 erected the city's largest church, according to official chronicles.

Novgorod occupies an important place in Russian political history as well. In 862 it was conquered and made the capital of the Viking prince Rurik, whose heirs founded the Kievan dynasty and ruled most of European Russia until 1598. More important,

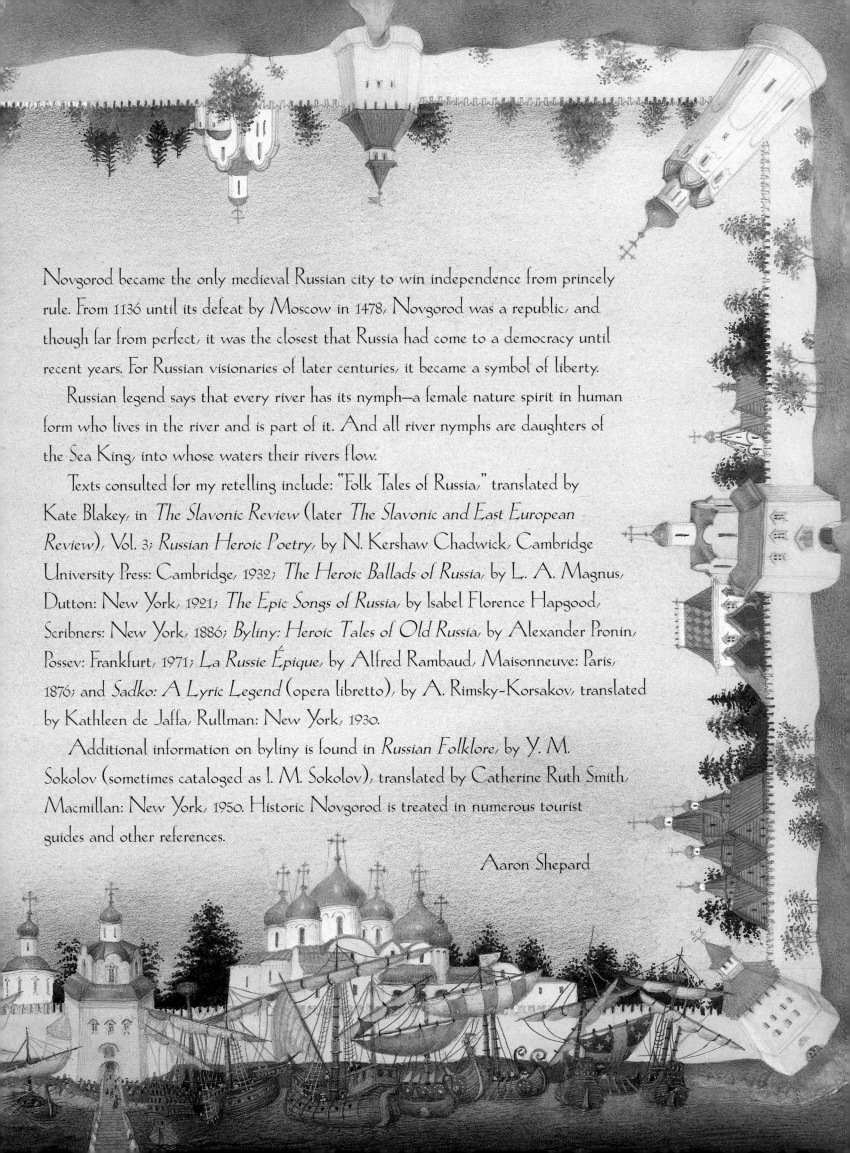

Novgorod became the only medieval Russian city to win independence from princely rule. From 1136 until its defeat by Moscow in 1478, Novgorod was a republic, and though far from perfect, it was the closest that Russia had come to a democracy until recent years. For Russian visionaries of later centuries, it became a symbol of liberty.

Russian legend says that every river has its nymph—a female nature spirit in human form who lives in the river and is part of it. And all river nymphs are daughters of the Sea King, into whose waters their rivers flow.

Texts consulted for my retelling include: "Folk Tales of Russia," translated by Kate Blakey, in *The Slavonic Review* (later *The Slavonic and East European Review*), Vol. 3; *Russian Heroic Poetry*, by N. Kershaw Chadwick, Cambridge University Press: Cambridge, 1932; *The Heroic Ballads of Russia*, by L. A. Magnus, Dutton: New York, 1921; *The Epic Songs of Russia*, by Isabel Florence Hapgood, Scribners: New York, 1886; *Byliny: Heroic Tales of Old Russia*, by Alexander Pronin, Possev: Frankfurt, 1971; *La Russie Épique*, by Alfred Rambaud, Maisonneuve: Paris, 1876; and *Sadko: A Lyric Legend* (opera libretto), by A. Rimsky-Korsakov, translated by Kathleen de Jaffa, Rullman: New York, 1930.

Additional information on byliny is found in *Russian Folklore*, by Y. M. Sokolov (sometimes cataloged as I. M. Sokolov), translated by Catherine Ruth Smith, Macmillan: New York, 1950. Historic Novgorod is treated in numerous tourist guides and other references.

Aaron Shepard

Special thanks to Daniel Hendrick, Ilya Spirin, and Roman Yangarber for their assistance.

Atheneum Books for Young Readers
An imprint of Simon & Schuster Children's Publishing Division
1230 Avenue of the Americas
New York, New York 10020

Book design by Michael Nelson
The text of this book is set in Eva Antiqua LtSg.
The illustrations are rendered in watercolor and colored pencil.

First Edition
Printed in Hong Kong by South China Printing Co. (1988) Ltd.
10 9 8 7 6 5 4 3 2 1

Library of Congress Cataloging-in-Publication Data
Shepard, Aaron.
The sea king's daughter : a Russian legend / retold by Aaron Shepard ; illustrated by Gennady Spirin.
p. cm.
Summary: A talented musician from Novgorod plays so well that the Sea King
wants him to marry one of his daughters.
ISBN 0-689-80759-7
[1. Folklore—Russia.] I. Spirin, Gennadii, ill. II. Title.
PZ8.1.S53945Se 1997
398.2 0947 01—dc20
[E] 96-3391